Written by Honey Henry

Unicorn Princess

Illustrated by Neville Henry

AuthorHouse™ UK
1663 Liberty Drive
Bloomington, IN 47403 USA
www.authorhouse.co.uk
Phone: 0800.197.4150

Published by AuthorHouse   04/05/2018

ISBN: 978-1-5462-8618-9 (sc)
ISBN: 978-1-5462-8617-2 (e)

authorHOUSE®

Chapter 1

Ralinyan

Far, far away, there is a secret land called Ralinyan that no human knows about; it's so secret in fact, I can't tell you the location, however it's the most magical place you could ever want to visit. It's filled with good magic and happiness, rainbows and blue skies. But who exactly lives here, you may wonder. Well, unicorns and their cousins, the pegasus. Yep. That's right. Pegasus and unicorns are real. They aren't just mythical creatures in fairy stories. As a matter of fact, I'm a unicorn myself. We don't quite know how humans even had an idea of us existing, but as long as there is no actual proof of our existence, then everything is ok. Happy, happy, happy, you may think, but unfortunately not. Despite almost all pegasus and unicorns being the most loving creatures, there are evil unicorns, who are currently trying to take over our land. But why exactly are these unicorns evil? Well, it all started centuries ago, when the evil witches were existing; these wicked creatures put a spell on the innocent unicorns, attempting to turn them into their evil slaves, but the unicorns turned so evil and rebellious, they tried to attack the witches, as well as all the good creatures, however, the witches escaped and nobody has seen them since. Luckily, despite the witches's evil efforts to put a spell on all unicorns, and all pegasus, many of us escaped, but the spell has remained generations later, being inherited by all offspring of these cursed creatures. Unfortunately, there is nothing we can do to help them. We could kill off all the cursed unicorns, but two wrongs don't make a right, and deep down they're good - it's just buried under the spell. However, until we find a cure, the evil unicorns could potentially turn everyone else in this land evil, but not only that, they could turn the whole universe evil!

Chapter 2

Cure of evil

Queen Rosaline is the queen of this land, and she is also my mother, making me Princess Diamond of Ralinyan. She is the most beautiful creature you'll ever know. Her body is a pure and heavenly shade of white, her mane and tail are a glistening gold, and her emerald eyes contrast so well. Not only is she the most beautiful creature, she is the most powerful too. She has the horn of a unicorn, and the wings of a pegasus, yet her horn has twice the power of a regular unicorn, and her wings can fly twice as fast as a regular pegasus. Then why can't she just turn all the evil unicorns good again, you may wonder, well, she hasn't quite got the power to do that, and besides, it's way to risky: one strike of evil power, and my beloved mother is dead! The thought of it brings tears to my eyes. Every other unicorn will just become evil, but Queen Rosaline has too much love in her heart to ever become evil. Obviously Queen Rosaline is the queen of the good creatures, but who is the queen of the evil?

Queen Raven. Queen of evil. She's the most wicked creature you'll ever know. Her body is a dim grey colour, her mane, tail, wings and horn filled with evil magic are dark purple, and her eyes are completely black. Her colours are as dark as her intentions. Firstly, she wants to kill Queen Rosaline, then she wants to turn every creature in this land evil, and take all their power, she then wants to kill every plant, get rid of the sunlight, turn all water into goo, and so on. Once she has completed this land, she wants to do it to the rest of the universe! To prevent this from happening, we put up a wall of love. It's a shield that will prevent any evil creature from entering our land. Then what do we have to worry about? Well, the shield can only last for a certain amount of time, and it takes up too much power to just do another one. Finding a solution sounds hopeless, right? Wrong! Fortunately, I know a wizard that may be able to help. He's our only hope, so I really, really, really hope he can.

Wizard Radigast is the most powerful wizard on this land - he's the only one who might be able to make a potion to cure the evil unicorns. I rush to tell my mum. Even though I live in the palace, I can't help but stop to admire it. It's so tall, its intimidating, so shiny, it's blinding. It's gold and white, matching my mum perfectly. The palace is bordered by loads of guards. I walk through never-ending hallways, up and down staircases as tall as mountains, and in and out rooms, trying to find my mother. She ended up being at the very top of the palace, looking sad and hopeless, as if she was about to cry, but she held the tears back. The door was open, but I still knock.

"Excuse me, mum?" I say.

I didn't bother asking what the matter was - it was obvious.

"Yes dear?" She replied. Her voice was shaking

"I have thought of a way we could cure the evil unicorns" I said.

"There isn't a way darling. It's hopeless!" She said.

"I think there is." I said.

"Ok, go on." She sighed

"We could ask Wizard Radigast to make us a potion." I said excitedly.

"He's miles away! And besides he might not even be able to help!" She cried.

"We must try! We have nothing to lose!" I argued

"Yes but-"

"No buts! We must try to save our land. I thought you of all creatures would agree, but if you don't then I'll do it myself!" I interrupted. I can't believe I just snapped at my mum (the queen). She looked at me in shock, not knowing what to say.

"Very well. We shall contact Wizard Radigast, asking him for help." Said my mum

Chapter 3

Life-saving letter

Dear Wizard Radigast,

I am writing in regards to a much needed cure.
Is there any way you can turn evil unicorns good again?
If so, please respond as soon as you can.

Kind regards,
Queen Rosaline of Ralinyan

That's the letter my mum wrote to Wizard Radigast. I just hope Wizard Radigast has a cure.

Luckily, he responded the next day. As my mum read the letter, her eyes lit up, like stars twinkling in the sky, but she suddenly looked confused.

Dear Queen Rosaline,

If you could bring me the following ingredients, I shall happily see what I can do:

1 happiness
2 kindnesses
3 loves

Once you have these, bring them to the other side of the rainbow, across the lake, and along the pathway.

Kind Regards,
Wizard Radigast

"How are we supposed to bring him one happiness, two kindnesses and three loves?" Exclaimed mum

"I don't know, but there must be a way." I said.

Chapter 4

The first riddle

Mum and I sat down, thinking long and hard, trying to unravel the riddle Wizard Radigast had given us. After ages of thinking, we decided to look in the great library for clues. I came across a book about the tree of happiness. It looked like any old tree, but it must have something special. I continued reading, and found out that all fairies are born there. When a baby first laughs, a flower opens from this tree, and pop! Out comes a fairy. This must be the answer, yet I was still confused. I hand mum the book.

"How can we bring Wizard Radigast the whole tree?" I asked

"Of course we aren't going to bring the entire tree. We'll bring a stick from it." Replied mum

Now it all made sense. One stick of happiness. Mum and I set off on our journey. It was an awfully long one - we had to go to Zalinix, the land which the fairies lived in. We've been flying for hours on end, and it was getting to much. I could see Zalinix in the distance. Just a few more flaps of my wings. I was breathing so heavily, because of how exhausted I was. Just one more..just one- I suddenly found I wasn't flapping my wings anymore. I was falling! I desperately tried to flap my wings, but I just fell lower and lower. I then felt something warm and silky underneath me, saving me from falling. It was my mum! She saved my life!

"We have arrived at Zalinix." She said, in her comforting voice, gently landing on the beach.

"Thank you." Is all I managed to squeeze out, but if I wasn't as tired, and hadn't almost died, I could've said a speech about how grateful I was. We stayed on that beach for the night. Before I knew it, it was morning. I was woken up by a beautiful melody, but I didn't know where it was coming from. To my surprise mum was awake.

"Who was singing that beautiful melody?" I asked

"I don't know, but it seems to be coming from the sea." Replied mum

I approach the sea, following the trail of the melody. As I got closer, it got louder. I suddenly could see a beautiful creature I had never seen before. It had the face and upper body of a women but the fins of a fish! It was a mermaid!

I had never seen one before, I had only ever heard legends about them. I didn't just see one mermaid, I found a whole bunch of them, all singing together, harmonising perfectly. One of them turned around and saw me. I thought she was going to get angry at me for spying

on them, but she just smiled and waved. I smiled back. Another signalled for me to come over. I couldn't swim, so entering the sea would be dangerous, but as long as I remain on the shallow end, it'll be ok. And besides, how could I resist? They were so beautiful! They all had different colour fins, but every one was a perfect shade. Their hair was so long and thick, trailing past their waists. They all looked so different. Some had brown hair, some had blonde some had pale skin, some had dark, but what they did have in common was their beauty. They wore strings of pearls around their waists, and a tiara of shells, pearls, and seaweed. I called mum over, and together we went towards the mermaids. Out of nowhere, the mermaids splash us! This doesn't sound like much of a problem, but if our wings get wet, we can't fly for the next thirty minutes! To prevent any more problems, mum and I attempt to gallop away, but the mermaids grab our legs and drag us deeper into the water. They're surprisingly strong. I manage

to kick one of the mermaid's tiaras off, meaning she had to get it before it sunk to the bottom of the ocean. While she was busy rummaging around, I quickly galloped onto the shore, but mum was still stuck. I desperately tried to drag her onto the shore, but if I got to close, the mermaids will drag me in again. Just as she was about to drown, a dolphin came and bashed the mermaids out of the way.

Mum quickly galloped onto the shore. I was shocked at how creatures so beautiful could be so cruel. In a way, they weren't beautiful at all. Their faces were attractive, but they were cruel creatures, and if you've got a horrible personality, then who cares if you have nice features? I guess you can never judge a book by it's cover.

"Thank you so much!" Mum and I said

"No problem!" Replied the dolphin, beginning to swim off.

"Wait!" I called

"Yes?" Said the dolphin

"Do you know where the tree of kindness is?" I asked

"Fly over the volcano, go under the waterfall, go across the field with yellow flowers, and you'll see the tree standing on it's own." Said the dolphin

"Thank you." Mum and I said

We rested and dried off in the scorching sun. In the distance, I could see the smoke from the volcano. Just the thought of a volcano scared me, and soon I had to fly over one but it had to be done, and sometimes we have to face our fears. Mum and I flew towards the volcano. It was a surprisingly long journey, even though the volcano seemed so close. As we got closer, it got hotter. The temperature went from cold, to warm, to hot. Mum said we now had to fly higher, because of how hot it was. I looked down, and saw the volcano underneath me. I could also feel the heat underneath me. Lava oozed out of the volcano, slithering like a snake, slowly making its way down the volcano. As the lava bubbled out the volcano, sparks came out as well, twinkling like stars. It was a scary, yet beautiful sight. A sight I had never seen before. The colours were so vibrant. The lava was a reddish orange, and the sparks were a goldish yellow. It was an image I could never forget. Before I knew it, that beautiful sight, those amazing colours, were a fraction of my imagination. I had done it. I had flown over a volcano. I had faced my fear. We land, but I don't feel the warm sand on my hooves, nor is the sea in sight. We are no longer on the beach. Instead we're in some weird forest. It has many trees but it also has a lake.

"Let's get a drink from the lake" said mum

I follow her as she trots to the lake.

"How are we going to find a waterfall? It could be anywhere!" I said

"Luckily, I know some creatures who can help" Replied mum

"Who?" I asked. I was quite confused

"The centaurs. They're relatives of ours."

She neighed loudly, and suddenly these creatures came trotting over. They had the upper body of men, but the rest of them was a horse. Although they had no horn or wings, they were part horse so they were clearly relatives, (any horse related animal are related to unicorns and pegasus) however, I'd never even heard of them. They looked ever so majestic, but also quite intimidating. Every centaur towered over both me and mum. They could easily run us over, but surprisingly, they were really nice.

"Your majesty!" Said one of the centaurs, dipping his head in respect

"How may I serve you, your highness?" Said another, kneeling down

"Do you know of any waterfalls around here?" Asked my mum

"Yes your majesty. Follow us." Replied one of the centaurs

The centaur's voices were deep and rough, but they spoke so kindly. Mum and I followed the centaurs. They were only walking, but since they're so big, we had to trot to keep up. It was exhausting, but since it meant we were one step closer to saving the universe, it was worth it. Soon I could hear the sound of water, and I knew we had reached the waterfall at last. I look up and there it is. The water glistens in the sunlight, as it trickles down onto the lake, making a soothing noise. As beautiful as it looked, I didn't want to go anywhere near it, let alone underneath it. What if there are mermaids who drown me again? What if I can't get away this time? What if my wings never dry and I can never fly again? What if, is all that was going through my head. My fear was taking over and I couldn't bear it. I want to think of positive things but there are non, and I desperately want to believe there is enough time to save the universe from evil unicorns, but it's unrealistic. What if there simply isn't enough time. I want to give up and rest my scrawny little legs, far away from any water, far away from mermaids, far away from danger. I want to forget this whole plan. I want to wake up from this nightmare, but I'm not sleeping. Why can't I just turn back time and somehow prevent the witches from causing this. What if the potion doesn't even work? I done it again. What if. But what if I give up now and let the evil unicorns take over. I need to give myself a chance, and even if there is no way out of this problem, at least I tried everything I could to save the universe.

"Here is the waterfall, your majesty." Said one of the centaurs

"Thank you." Mum and I said

"Any time your majesty." Said the centaurs

"You don't happen to be going to the tree of kindness, do you? Said one of the centaurs

"You guessed it." Mum said

"The tree will be guarded by the fairies, and to get past them, you will need to bring them a gift." Explained the centaur

"What kind of gift?" Asked mum

"A feather from the golden eagle. The real golden eagle. The one on earth is fake, the real golden eagle lives here."

"How are we supposed to get a feather from it?" Asked mum

"I'll get it." Said the centaur

We waited for a bit, and then out came this glistening bird. It shone like the sun, showing off it's gold feathers. It was the golden eagle, confidently sitting on a branch, it's head up high. It looked so rare. So magical. Although they're probably quite common, since we didn't have to wait for long before it came out. The centaur held his arrow high, and with perfect aim he shot down the beautiful bird. I feel tears sting my eyes. I'm being stupid. Dramatic. I don't even know the bird. I had never even heard of the species. No. That's not the point. That bird was a living creature. It's life may not have mattered to us, but it still had one. I feel a sensation of rage flow through my body. I feel more tears fill my eyes, until everything becomes a blur.

"How could you carelessly take a life like that? Don't you have any consideration?" I shout, without thinking
"How dare you speak to anybody like that, let alone the one who is helping us!" Shouted my mum, now also in a

rage, but I didn't care. Her voice was getting quieter in my mind, because I simply wasn't listening.

"The bird can be killed 200 times, and wake up unharmed, your majesty." Said the centaur

I feel relieved, but soon that feeling of relief is taken over by embarrassment. I feel queasy. It tickles, but in a way that it makes me want to throw up. I stare at that golden eagle. My mind blank. The image goes blurry as the centaur trots over to the golden eagle and plucks a feather from it, then hands it to my mum.

"Thank you." Said my mum

"Anytime your majesty." Said the centaur

"Come on Diamond! I'm appalled at your rudeness!" Said mum

I obey her, and trot forward, closer to the waterfall. I hold my breath, and close my eyes. I feel the cold water on my body, sending shivers down my spine. It was a horrible, yet refreshing feeling. I hated it. No. I loved it. It's hard to explain. I keep trotting, and I'm out of the water. I see topaz flowers on an emerald field. It was the field of yellow flowers.

I smelt a beautiful aroma as soon as I stepped on the first blade of grass. It was amazing.

"I'm sorry mum." I mumbled

"It's not me who you should be saying sorry to it's that poor centaur. Just don't do it again." Said mum

"Ok" I said

Mum and I ran freely through the beautiful field, as the cool breeze brushed my golden mane, showing it off, creating a perfect image. We kept running, and I loved it. I wanted it to last forever, but obviously that couldn't happen, because the tree of happiness was right in front of me. I felt a sudden sting on my body. It was one of the fairies protecting the tree. There were hundreds of them, yet non of them were like how I imagined. They all had brightly coloured body suits, and neatly cut hair.

"Who are you, and why are you here?" Questioned the fairy in a serious tone, but her voice was so squeaky and high pitched, and she was so tiny that I could stamp on her, I couldn't help but laugh a little. She stung me again, now with an angry look on her face.

"We are sorry to disturb you, but we are wondering if we could have a stick from your tree. We have brought you a gift in return." Said mum, holding the golden eagle feather in her teeth.

"Deal." Said the fairy, looking at the feather suspiciously. She then broke off the skinniest twig from the tree, handed it to me and snatched the feather from my mum. I felt so happy. We had completed the first quest. Now we have to get two kindnesses. Somehow.

The second riddle

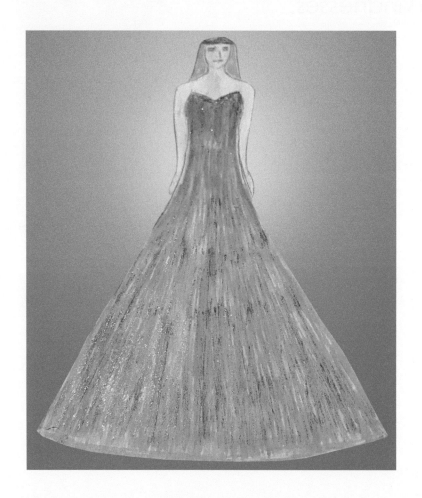

"What is meant by two kindnesses?" I asked

"I don't know, but I do know of an act of kindness." Replied mum

"What is it?" I asked curiously

"Well, have you ever wondered who your father is?" Asked mum

"Yes, but it's never really bothered me." I said

"His name is King Leo of Ralinyan. He was an extremely kind and brave unicorn. He sacrificed his life for us. When you were just a young foal, Queen Raven was attacking me, and just as the fire was about to hit me, he stood in the line of the fire so it hit him instead. You and I escaped, but your father didn't. This all happened in the palace gardens, and ever since, beautiful golden flowers have grown there, so if we pick one of those flowers, it should be one of the answers." Explained mum. Tears filled her eyes, but she blinked them away. I suddenly got a flashback. A ball of fire and a scream. It was very vague, but it seemed so familiar, now that mum had told me. Tears filled my eyes now, and I tried to blink them away, but they just rolled down my cheek.

"Are you ok Diamond?" Asked mum

"Yes mum, I'm fine." I lied. The flashback replayed in my head, but it eventually faded away.

"So all we have to do is pick a flower from the palace gardens, and mission complete?" I asked, shocked, but relieved

"Well yes, but I don't know how to get the second kindness." Said mum, but I tried not to worry about the second kindness just yet.

We went to the palace gardens, and there were thousands of shimmering, gold flowers. I picked one. I got another flashback, and an image of my father swam through my head. He was pure white, with a few gold streaks in his mane. He looked so noble, but the image only lasted a second. I missed him all of a sudden. It was as if I had known him my whole life, yet I didn't even know his name until now. I didn't care until now. I suddenly felt strong feelings of love, compassion, and desperation, but how can I love someone I barely know or remember? I so badly wanted him to be here with me. I wanted him to be on this mission with me. I trotted away before I started crying again.

"Where on Ralinyan are we going to find the second kindness?" I asked

"Well, I don't think it's going to be on Ralinyan at all." Said mum

"Where then?" I asked

"You're going to have to travel to earth." Said mum

"Yay! I've always wanted to go to earth!" I said in excitement

"Wait, but where exactly am I going to go?" I asked

"To the fields of Northern France, where soldiers sacrificed their lives in World War 1. There's a story that thousands of soldiers died there, and these red flowers called poppies grew there after the war, so if you pick one of these flowers, it should be the second kindness. I don't know how true this story is, but it's worth a try." Explained mum

"But how can I go to earth if I'm a unicorn?" I asked

"You're not going to be a unicorn." Said mum, but before I could say anything more, she turned me into a beautiful human princess using the magic of her horn. I had long blonde hair, with distinctive gold streaks, matching my shimmering gold dress. I had emerald green eyes and rosy pink lips. I couldn't believe that I'm actually a human! I had diamond earrings, a diamond necklace and a diamond tiara to match my name. I twirled around and hugged mum. I still had the powers of a unicorn, but they had to be kept hidden as soon as I landed on earth.

"The spell only lasts 24 hours, so you must be back within this time." Said mum

"Wait, how am I even going to get to earth if I don't have wings anymore?" I asked

"You can teleport yourself." Said mum

"How?" I said

"Close your eyes and think of where you want to teleport to. Good luck." Said mum. It was the 11th day of the 11th month, the same day WW1 ended. I did as mum said, and closed my eyes. I imagined a field full of ruby red poppies. I opened my eyes and there I was. The scent was so strong, and the colours were so much more vibrant than I imagined. I picked one, but there's so much more time, and I need to make the most of it. I suddenly remembered a story of a princess named Lydia. She was known as the princess of kindness. I needed to visit her while I was still on earth. I close my eyes, and think deeply of Princess Lydia but something doesn't feel right. I open my eyes and I'm in these large hallways, but nobody else is there. I see a statue of Princess Lydia, and realise it's a memorial. Princess Lydia is dead. My heart sank. Underneath her statue, there was a book which told of her legacy. I found that her greatest passion was to help others, so she set up a charity. Since I had no money, I donated my diamond necklace. I wandered the eerie hallways, in hope to find someone. All of a sudden, a handsome young man appeared behind me.

"Excuse me madam." He said

"Yes?" I replied

"Have you mislaid your necklace?" He asked, holding up my diamond necklace

"No, I wanted to donate it to Princess Lydia's charity." I said

"That's most generous of you! As it happens, I am hosting a ball tonight to fundraise for my mother's charity, and it would honour me if you should attend." He said

"Yes, I would love to!" I said excitedly

"So where are you staying?" Asked the prince

"I've only just arrived." I said

"Well would you care to have lunch with me?" Asked the prince

"I would love to!" I said

The prince and I had the most amazing feast, and he then took me on a tour of the palace. I thought my palace was huge, but it's nothing in comparison to the prince's palace. We ended the tour in the palace gardens. It was an endless field with thousands of colourful flowers. We both shared the love of flowers, and of each other. As we sat in the rose gardens, the prince leant forward and kissed me. It was then I knew I had fallen for him, and it was obvious he felt the same. We spent the rest of the day together, talking about our lives, childhoods, and passions, and although it had only been a day we had spent together, it felt as if we'd spent a year together. Before we knew it, it was evening, and time for the ball. The prince had insisted the first dance to be with me. Everybody surrounded us, and watched as we danced. It felt amazing as I glided across the floor. After the dance, we sat down and had a drink.

"It's as if we've met before." Said the prince

"We couldn't have." I said, although I also felt a strong sense of deja vu

"How can you be so certain?" Asked the prince

"Because it's impossible." I said, awkwardly

"I must leave, but I promise I will return and explain." I said

"Why? Where will you go?" Said the prince

"I can't tell you right now." I said

"For this relationship to work, you need to tell me." Said the prince, beginning to lose his patience

I ignored him, and ran off to the palace gardens, disappearing into the darkness. The prince tried to follow me, but he got caught up in the crowd. I closed my eyes and teleported back to Ralinyan. Not long after, I changed back into a unicorn, and gave the poppy to mum. I strongly missed the prince, but I pushed him to the back of my mind, because although I promised to see him again, I was unsure how true that promise was, yet it was quite strange, because we seemed to meet in our dreams that night.

Chapter 6

The third riddle

The next day, mum and I were working on the third riddle: 3 loves. Luckily, mum had an idea of what the answer could be. She told me a legend about my great great great grandfather, who had paid a ransom of three large gems to an evil rival for the release of his love, who he later married. He did this out of his love for the princess, which is why they're known as the gems of love. He placed the gems at the entrance of the cave, and when his rival released the princess, and went over to the gems, the dragon who lived in the cave came out and ate him. The gems have remained there ever since, and so has the dragon.

"We need to travel to the cave. It's not too far away, so it should be a pretty easy journey." Said mum

We soon arrived at the cave, and we needed to think

of a way we could trick the dragon, into coming out of his cave. We decided that mum would distract the dragon, since she's the fastest of all unicorns, and I'll sneak in, and attempt to take the gems. I hid closely to the cave. Mum made lots of noise near the entrance of the cave, and soon the dragon came out and tried to eat her, I so badly wanted to come out and attack the dragon, but I knew I must stay hidden. The dragon blew fire at mum, but she dodged and flew away. The dragon flew after her. I came out of my hiding place, and entered the cave. There were many skeleton bones scattered around. The cave was dark, and was therefore difficult to walk around. I stumbled down further into the cave, searching for the gems. I then noticed a light in the distance. The light was coming from a gap between two stones. I pushed one of the stones aside, realising it was a lid. Inside the stone was the three gems, amongst a huge amount of treasure. There were gold bars, gold chains, diamonds, pearls, and many other gemstones. The three gems of love were very distinctive. They were ruby, emerald, and sapphire gems, all the same size, together, in an open box. Although I was tempted to take lots of other treasures as well, I only picked up the box of the gems of love. I hurried back to the entrance of the cave. Meanwhile, mum was having a difficult time with the dragon, since the dragon was also fast at flying, but it was not as agile as my mum. Mum flew in and out of the trees, whilst the dragon blew fire at her. She could feel the flames, and knew she could not get away for much longer, and decided the only way she's going to get away is if she flew vertically, as fast as she could. The dragon chased her, but couldn't blow flames at her. Although she was very tired, she knew she was flying for her life. The dragon was gaining on her. She flew so high, the oxygen was low, and she began to feel faint. She knew she had to keep going. The dragon fainted, and began to fall to the ground. Mum also fainted, and fell to the ground. The dragon regained consciousness, near the ground. It flapped it's wings, trying to fly, but hit the ground hard, and injured one of it's wings. It was unable to fly, but blew great amounts of fire up at mum, who was still falling. She tried to flap her wings, and prevent herself from falling. She could feel the heat from the flames, as it singed her wings. She flapped as hard as she could, and then flew horizontally, away from the dragon. I came out of the cave, as mum was flying away. I followed her with the three gems of love. The dragon was raging, and blew great amounts of fire, burning down the forest. It was a difficult, and painful journey for mum, but at least we had the three gems of love.

The great wizard

We went back to the palace, and I tended to mum's wounds. We needed to rest, so we slept at the palace for the night. The next day we set off on our journey, to wizard Radigast. We had to go to the other side of the rainbow, across the lake, and along the pathway. These were the instructions on the letter he sent us, and even though they seemed  pretty straight forward, mum and I were confused as to what rainbow, since it could be any rainbow in the world. We went to the library for clues. I found a book about all the great things which are only found in Ralinyan. Luckily, one of these things was a rainbow that was always there, and has been there since the beginning of time, but this wasn't the only special thing about it. Unlike normal rainbows, there was an end to it, yet nobody ever dared travel to that end, because rumour has it, once you travel to that end, you can never come back, but mum and I had to take that risk. Hopefully, this is the rainbow wizard Radigast meant. It wasn't too far from the palace, so it was easy to get there. Once we had arrived, there was no question. The colours were so bright, it was as if they glowed. The red glistened like a ruby, the orange and yellow shone like the sun, the green was as bold as the grass, the blue was as deep as the sea, and the indigo and violet were unexplainable. Not only did the fluorescent colours amaze me, but so did the size of the rainbow. It seemed to go right through the clouds. I placed my hoof on the rainbow, and found out that it was solid, so we could trot across it like a bridge, which was great, because mum struggled to fly due to her injuries. Mum and I stepped on the rainbow, and began to canter across it. It was an amazing feeling, but also quite scary as we got higher up, except I wasn't scared for my self. If I fall, I'll just fly back up. I was scared for mum. What if she fell, and couldn't fly back up, and the thought of that rumour was scary, but I tried not to think about either of them, because I was having so much fun. I glided through the clouds, and everything below me looked so small. It was a long journey, but I somehow managed to canter my way through it all, without a problem. We finally reached the end of the rainbow, and the rumour turned out to be nothing more than lie. At least for now. The other end of the rainbow was a desolate field. We searched for a bit, and soon found a lake. I was surprised at how easy that was, considering all the challenges we had to face before. I was surprised but relieved, except that didn't last for long, because I suddenly remembered mum's injuries. How was she supposed to fly across? There were no other options than fly, because neither of us could swim. Before, she could effortlessly glide along, for miles and miles, but now look. Look what that evil beast did to my beloved mother. Her wings are burnt because of that monster. She acted brave, but I knew she was crying inside. I wanted to pretend that everything was ok, and I'm quite sure mum does to, because she hasn't once spoke of her injuries, or that evil, sinister dragon. Maybe she doesn't want me to worry. I need to stop thinking about it, because every time I get more and more angry at the monster who caused it, and I'm going to end up- I realised I was thinking out loud. I took a deep breath and calmed down.

"Mum, how are you going to fly across the lake?" I asked

"Like I usually do." Said mum. It was as if her injuries had disappeared, and she had not a clue why I would ask such a stupid question. I wish. I glance over at her wings, and they're still burnt.

"But your injuries." I mumble

"So? It's going to cause me a lot of pain to fly across the river, and I mean a lot. It's going to be a challenge, but I'm not going to let some stupid injuries from some pathetic dragon stop me from doing what I want to do." Said mum.

She flew across the river, and although she acted confident, it was obvious how much she struggled. It was painful to watch her in pain. She struggled deeply, but she still done it. She believed she could, so she did. I followed her, lost for words. All we had to do now is trot along the pathway. It was a tree lined pathway, and the trees arched in, creating a tunnel. At the end of the pathway, was a strange, little cottage, and outside the cottage was a funny looking man. It was wizard Radigast. I was so relieved. It was as if he was waiting for us. It was like he knew we were coming just then. He greeted us with open arms.

"Welcome!" He said joyfully

He was a very strange man, but ever so kind. He wore a mauve cloak that had a yellow stripe running down the middle, and a matching pointy hat. His beard looked like it had been grown for years, yet it had not a strand of colour. It was pure white. His cottage looked old and battered, and had ivy crawling all over it. Outside, near to where he was standing was a big black cauldron.

"Queen Rosaline and Princess Diamond, am I right?" Asked Wizard Radigast

"Yes. Here are the ingredients." Said mum, handing them over

"Wonderful." Said Wizard Radigast joyfully

Wizard Radigast poured some clear liquid into the cauldron, then added the three gems of love. The mixture began to bubble as he mixed it with the stick of happiness. He then added the two flowers of kindness and it turned bright, fluorescent green as he mixed it some more. He then asked us to dip our horns in the potion. We obeyed this instruction, and the potion absorbed into our horns, turning them bright, fluorescent green.

"There's only enough for two strikes each. They can be used to take a life or give a life. The effect is determined by your heart's intention." Explained Wizard Radigast

"Thank you." Mum and I said

Chapter 8

Tale of two queens

We returned home, only to witness the destruction the evil unicorns had caused. The shield of love was wearing off, and the evil unicorns were taking over. The land was covered by thunderclouds and darkness, and the rivers were a pile of goo, but I used this destruction as motivation. Mum and I came up with a plan. We went to the great hall, yet not to hide. We wanted Queen Raven to notice us so she'll also come to the great hall and we can destroy her, and turn everything back to normal. Soon we caught her attention, and she galloped into the great hall. As soon as she entered, the doors were locked, so nobody could enter. The great hall was covered in mirrors, so Queen Raven could not tell which was mum's reflection, and which one was actually her. I hid so Queen Raven couldn't see me. All of a sudden, Queen Raven started flying really fast, shooting at the mirrors, smashing them to pieces. She done this to find out where mum was. Mum shot at Queen Raven but missed. Queen Raven stopped and took aim at mum, as she now knew where she was. They both shot at each other, at exactly the same time, neither missed, but Queen Raven was only grazed, whereas mum fell to the ground dying. Queen Raven reared up and let out an evil laugh.

"Hahahahahahaha the kingdom is mine!" Bellowed Queen Raven

How could I just sit and watch as my mother dies? I would've killed this beast ages ago if mum had let me fight her. I came out of my hiding place and shot Queen Raven straight in the heart. She exploded into a million crystal pieces. I ran over to mum, and she looked like she was dead - no she couldn't be.

"Mum!" I yell

No response

"Mum!" I yell, even louder

Still no response. She was dead. I feel empty all of a sudden. It was like my heart had been ripped out. Tears streamed down my face uncontrollably. Without me realising, potion from my horn dripped down onto mum. Suddenly, she opened her eyes.

"Mum, you're alive!" I yell joyfully

She looked refreshed, and her injuries had healed!

"My darling!" She replied and we embraced.

We exited the great hall, out into the open space of Ralinyan. Everything turned back to normal. The grey thunderclouds faded away, revealing the shining sun. The rivers of goo changed from horrible green slop into crystal clear aqua, and the evil unicorns turned from pure grey into black, white, brown, and many other colours, yet it was more than their colour that was changing. They were changing from evil to good. I suddenly felt slightly guilty. I didn't care one bit about Queen Raven, but unicorns aren't meant to kill one another. Was it really the only way?

"Mum, unicorns aren't meant to kill anyone, so why did we have to kill Queen Raven? I really don't care, but I thought unicorns are against violence." I said

"Queen Raven wasn't real. She was created by the witches to lead the evil unicorns, hence the reason she shattered into a million crystal pieces." Said mum

Ralinyan is finally back to normal. Everything had gone to plan. Had it? I was so happy, but I then remembered something. Someone, actually. The prince. I promised I would return.

Chapter 9

No going back

"Mum, there's something you should know." I said

"What is it darling?" Asked mum

"When I went to earth a met a prince."

"Oh that's nice dear." Said mum, not seeming to take much interest

"He's the love of my life, and I promised I would return. Can I return to earth and see him? Please mum?" I asked

"Ok, but make sure you're back within 24 hours. Be careful." Said mum as she turned me into a human.

I teleported to earth, and went straight to the prince. As soon as I arrived the prince hugged me. I hugged him back. He seemed to never let go, and I didn't want him to. It was clearly a mutual feeling.

"Oh Diamond! Where have you been? You said you'll explain." Said the prince

I felt awkward. How could I explain that I was a unicorn?

"Do you believe in unicorns?" I asked

"There's many undiscovered creatures in this world. Why do you ask?" Said the prince

"Just hold my hand and close your eyes." I said

The prince did as I said, and when we opened our eyes we were in Ralinyan. The prince was very startled at first, because he was a unicorn. He was royalty, but not from Ralinyan, so he had a shiny silver mane.

"Mum, this is the prince I was talking about." I said

"Diamond, he's from earth! How could you let out the secret?" Said mum

"I trust him, and you trust me, don't you?" I said

Mum was silenced. I took the prince on a tour of the palace, and like on earth, we ended it in the palace gardens.

"So you really are a unicorn? How is this possible?" Said the prince

He seemed nervous and unsure, which was understandable.

"It just is." I replied

"Is it still possible for us to be together?" Asked the prince, looking quite worried

"Of course it is." I lied

How was it possible? I'm a unicorn, and he's a human, and I can change into a human, but only for 24 hours at a time. I acted as if we could definitely be together, because I didn't want to upset the prince. I didn't want to upset myself. I longed to be with him, but how? We were from completely different parts of the universe, and it's not like I can just move to earth as a unicorn, and let out the secret, so humans could come and hunt us down and the prince couldn't just leave his kingdom to live with a unicorn in another land. Who would believe him anyways? We went over to mum.

"Mum, is there anyway I could live with the prince?" I asked

"Well I guess so." Replied mum

I was celebrating inside, but mum didn't look so happy.

"You can either become a human for 24 hours, or become a human permanently. If you become a human permanently, you will lose all your powers, and you can only teleport once, which means you can never return to Ralinyan. This spell cannot be undone." Explained mum

I got a sudden flashback of my life at Ralinyan. How could I just leave my home and never come back? But the prince was the love of my life, and I knew if I lost him I'd regret it forever. I'd never loved someone like this. I'd never felt such a strong connection with another soul.

"Mum I want you to make me a human. Forever." I said
Tears filled my eyes but I knew this is what I wanted.

"Diamond are you sure? You do realise what you're doing, don't you?" Said mum

"Yes mum." I said

"I love you very, very much my little Diamond." Said mum, beginning to cry, and very few things made her cry too. "I love you to." I said, also crying, hugging mum

"Look after her." Mum said to the prince

Mum then turned us both into humans, and the prince and I then left Ralinyan, hand in hand.

When we got to earth, the prince proposed to me with the most beautiful ring. The band was yellow gold, and it had two small diamonds on the side, and one big diamond in the middle. They shone brighter than the sun. Obviously I accepted the prince's proposal. I met the king, and he gave us permission to marry.

"Son, I am going to be stepping down from the throne,

and you're next in line. See this as my wedding present." Said the king

The king then placed a beautiful tiara on my head as my wedding present, but marrying the prince was the only present I wanted. The king smiled. The prince said this was the first time he smiled since Princess Lydia's death. A few months later the prince and I got married. I wore a pure white dress with a 25ft long veil. As I walked down the isle, I noticed someone who looked familiar. She also looked a lot like me, except older and more mature. At the ball, I looked her in the eyes, and I instantly knew who it was.

"Mum is that you?" I said, running over to her

"Yes my darling. How could I miss such a special day?" She replied

I introduced her to the king, and they became great friends. Mum visited many times after our marriage, and we all lived happily ever after.

The end

Printed in the United States
By Bookmasters